SECRET PASSAGE

TOKI MATSUDAIRA

WORKBOOK PRESS LLC
187 E Warm Springs Rd,
Suite B285, Las Vegas, NV 89119, USA

Website: https://workbookpress.com/
Hotline: 1-888-818-4856
Email: admin@workbookpress.com

Ordering Information:
Quantity sales. Special discounts are available on quantity purchases by corporations, associations, and others.
For details, contact the publisher at the address above.

Library of Congress Control Number:

ISBN-13:   000-0-000000-00-0 (Paperback Version)
                000-0-000000-00-0 (Digital Version)

REV. DATE: 05/05/2022

Chapter 1

It was the 21ˢᵗ December 2018 in the evening that I heard the running footsteps of someone in a rush to get downstairs in my house. They seemed to be coming from nowhere. No sooner did I hear them, then the running feet suddenly stopped and there was quiet. I got up from the settee where I had been seated watching TV that evening, I went out of the room and checked the landing, the stairs , the kitchen and dining room below. I checked the bedrooms and bathrooms. There was nothing there. A little perplexed , I withdrew back into the TV room and continued watching television. After the movie had ended, I turned off the TV, left the room and made my way back to my own bedroom and to my own bed.

I was asleep for about one hour, I suddenly awakened aware of someone present in my room. I turned on the sidelight next to my bed but there was nobody there.I then turned off the bedside light, lay my head on the pillows and went back to sleep. When I woke up at 5am, I had a strange taste in my mouth, as if I had been eating something dis-tasteful. I climbed out of bed, turned on the bedroom light and went over to the long standing mirror. I took off my nightdress and inspected my body. I noticed marks around my hips which appeared to be shots caused by injections. I suddenly had to relieve myself and used the toilet. I noticed something wet in my groin. I had been unaware of the usage of rape on a sleeping woman. I guessed it was IRA Beth who had attacked me that night. I had had similar problems from her before when she wanted a lot of money from me. It wasn't so long ago, maybe two weeks that Beth had attacked some young children with an overdose of heroin killing most of them. There was no explanation of why she did this.

I heard the running occasionally during the day. They were at their strongest at night-time, especially when I was asleep. They kept waking me up. It occurred to me that there was an invisible passage leading into the house. I tried to find the opening for it but in my search, discovered nothing .I wanted to know who was there to disturb my sleep and my life like this. It was obvious to me that it was a drug related problem, by drug gangs trying to claim my property and assets. My former husband, now deceased became a drug dealer in his retirement. Those he left behind were after my money and my home. They were responsible for building the secret passage. This much I was able to guess. Jack and Sam, determined as ever to get hold of my money and my property held hostages often killing them. They worked for my husband when he was alive. It wouldn't be long now before a war would break in the very dangerous city that London was, possibly the most dangerous city in the world.

Chapter 2

Although Beth continued to harass me coming into my bedroom, Juanita Garcia, a big drug dealer from South America, was pushing hard to access my property and claim it with all it's contents. She wanted my money.

She took my security man, a Joe Harris, hostage and kidnapped him, taking him from the upstairs flat to her own house. She drugged him. When they arrived at her house, she put him to bed in a bedroom and forced more drugs into him. More security men came into the house and were told to sit down in a waiting room. They were drugged by her. Juanita left the room and when she came back she was like a wild animal. She had taken aphrodisiacs and leapt on the security man in bed and proceeded to have sex with him. She had raped him several times. For me, this was turning out to be the worst Christmas I had ever known. As crazy as all this sounds, it is all true. My deceased husband had left all this as his legacy to me. Luckily, there are no children.

The other person who never ceased to bother me was their Miss Stephanotis. She was an older terrorist with a lot of experience in terrorism. She was an err. One night she visited me in the TV room and tried to rape me, but because of the narrow arms of my armchair where I was sitting, she was too big and was unable to fit in between the narrow arms of the chair to grab some love from me.

She wanted me to give her over my home. She was fighting her war for this. She was a drug addict, addicted to heroin.Both Beth and Miss Stephanotis were able to fund their drug addiction and pay for the outgoings of their own flats. It was a myth that they had no money.

Then there were prostitutes and whores who worked for Juanita who came through the secret passage to look over my clothes and shoes. If ever I bought something new, they were the first to see them, and often going off with them! Beth often stole my clothes for terrorism in spite of the clothes not fitting her great height. Miss Stephanotis often had certain dresses of mine copied to fit her large size. After a while, I quit buying new clothes and shoes. Now I wear a lot of old clothes.

It was during this period of time that some inheritance money came into my account. It was held by my Trustees, in Jersey. A war eventually broke out for the money. Juanita decided she wanted the clean money for herself to give to her son.

My life was threatened. The secret passage was taken over by Juanita. She drugged the security man one day who was asleep in the secret flat attached to my house.

She kidnapped him taking him to her house in London. She put him to bed in one of her bedrooms and forced more drugs into his arm. More security men were brought into the house where they were told to sit in the waiting room. They too were shot in the arm by her and badly drugged. She then went back into her room where she took afrodisiacs and once it started working, she went back to Joe

Harris, still drugged in bed and started to rape him violently. She did this for over an hour. This happened on Christmas Day.

As I said before, all this is true and I repeat ,it must have been the worst Christmas I had ever had.

Chapter 3

A few days later, I was in my house. Outside, snow fell in the garden, streets and parks. Everything was covered under a blanket of snow. It continued to snow all morning. There was no sound and peace took over.

It turned 8am when I sat upright on my bed, watching the snow fall. I got out of bed and went downstairs to have breakfast. I prepared a coffee and opened the paper bag that held two croissants. It couldn't have been a nicer breakfast however fattening it was.

I was about to change and get ready for the day,when the doorbell rang. When I got to the door and opened it, there was nobody there. Annoyed, I closed the door and made my way upstairs again.

As I reached my bedroom, the doorbell rang again for the second time. I quickly descended the stairs and reached the front door, opening it quickly and saw Robert who forced his way in and closed the door. He took me in his arms and held me close, desperately kissing me! Taken aback, I was led into a bedroom and we both fell on the bed where he promptly undressed and went under the covers. He took off my dressing gown and started making love to me. I began to enjoy his love making.

After it was over, he asked me if he could have some breakfast. I led him downstairs and made some coffee for him and toasted some bread and fried eggs. He looked as if he hadn't eaten for a while and ate with a good appetite.

It continued to snow and I wondered if my appointment with the dentist was still on.

"What are your plans today," I asked him?

"My appointment has been cancelled because of the weather," he said.

"Transport hardly works and we are stuck, we won't be able to go anywhere today," he said.

He got up from the table and led me into the sitting room. He asked me to turn on the TV. We watched the news. The weather had caused severe disruption and roads were blocked. We must enjoy the snow outside whilst it lasts. They were expecting it to stop snowing this afternoon.

At this point, I excused myself and went to change my clothes. I got into a pair of ski trousers and pulled out a ski anorak and hat. I took out my fur boots and placed them near the front door. Then I went back to Robert who was vaguely watching television.

"Oh, you're all set for going out in the snow," he said.

"Yes, I thought we could go out for a little wander outside even though it is snowing quite heavily."

"I doubt I could come with you right now as I am wearing only trainers on my feet rather than snow boots I left at home. Why don't you go out alone for a few minutes and get some clean fresh air?" he asked.

"Tell me what your walk was like?" he added.

"I suppose that settles it" I said.

"Will you be alright watching TV?" I asked.

"I've done it before," he replied with a grin.

I gave him a kiss and returned to the hall where I had left my fur boots. As I was leaving I shouted "Bye. See you in a bit."

I opened the front door and saw a pile of snow on the walk way. However, it was not icy and powder snow did not threaten my walk. I walked slowly to the end of the street. I wore my goggles but found visibility difficult. It was snowing hard now. There wasn't a soul insight. No cars or buses passed by on the main road. One could have heard a pin drop, so quiet and peaceful was the street. It had gone 11.30am that morning. It was difficult to see anything except for a lot of snow so I decided to turn back. Suddenly, as I walked, I heard a loud noise coming from one of the houses on my left side. The security alarm which had been set up was ringing fiercely so I couldn't help but notice the house that it was coming from. It was my neighbour at No.45 whose alarm had been set off. I didn't know when they would return. I hastened my steps to get back home to telephone the police. When I got back, I realised I had been gone for about twenty five minutes. Kicking off my fur boots, I made for the telephone, called the Police to tell them at 45 Sinclair Parade, the security alarm had gone off. I explained I was a neighbour in the same street and had gone out into the snow for a short walk and returning to my house, the alarm had gone off. I didn't know when Reggie or Trevor would be back.

I am Olivia Warren. I live at No.32 Sinclair Parade in London, at Notting Hill. My beau is Robert. We have been together these past four years. We like each other a lot. Someday, we may marry. Until then, we will enjoy love with each other and have a lot of fun with each others' company.

Chapter 4

It continued to snow into the afternoon. Traffic had come to a standstill and Robert was forced to stay with me. His office in the city was closed. He was a stock broker. The running feet had stopped and there was peace in my house.

My neighbour from number 30 had let her young children out into their garden to make a snow man. Young Sandra worked hard on her snowman and her Mother had come outside to join her to help her make the snowman.

In the afternoon, I made some hot mulled wine which we drank enjoying the warming feeling of this hot drink. It was about 3 in the afternoon."Look, what a miracle, it's stopped snowing!" said Robert. "We can go out now. Let's take a walk after our drink."

"That's a brilliant idea, I said." A few minutes later, we bundled ourselves up and went outside. On our way to the top of Notting Hill, we momentarily stopped in front of number 43, as the alarm was still ringing. There wasn't anybody in sight. As we approached the road that led to the top of Notting Hill, we saw some children on their sleds speeding down the hill. They were screaming and laughing. All traffic had stopped and they had the hill to themselves.

We continued to climb up the hill and when we reached the top quite a number of children were preparing themselves and their sleds to whip down the hill. Very young children had to be accompanied by a parent and sit perched in the front of the sled with the parent navigating the direction of the sled.

We saw Martha and Jim and their little girl Emma. We went up to them "Hi, you're here too " I said. "We don't have a sled, but Emma is having a good time and loves the snow" said Jim. It was approaching 5 o'clock and getting dark. Robert and I decided to go home. We said our goodbye to the Cunninghams and made our way down the hill. The snow was powdery, not icy and we had little difficulty walking back home. As we approached Sinclair Parade it started to snow.. We hastened our steps until we reached my house. Once in the house, I flicked on the lights and Robert took off his trainers and socks and went around barefooted. I went to the spare room and opened the door of the linen closet. On the bottom shelf were a few old pair of men's socks once belonging to my father. I took out a pair and and went back to the hall and told Robert to try on "my father's socks." He tried them on and they fit him well enough. I took his own socks and trainers to the living room and turned on the gas fireplace putting the wet socks and trainers in front of it.

In the meanwhile, Robert had gone into the kitchen and was preparing a cocktail for the two of us. The vodka sour was delicious. I went briefly to the kitchen and put our dinner into the oven. It was a prepared dinner I had bought earlier on in the week. I drew the curtains in the drawing room. As I was doing this I saw that snow was still falling and wondered to myself if Robert would be stuck in my house again in the morning.

When the meal was ready we ate it in the kitchen.

I pulled out a bottle of French Bordeaux from the wine rack in the kitchen and opened it. I lit a candle on the table and dimmed the kitchen lights. It was a lovely dinner, one that I could never have imagined I would enjoy so much.

After clearing the table of plates and glasses, we were going to watch television. Just as I was about to leave the kitchen, Robert took me by the waist and gave me a big kiss holding me close to him. When he let go, I went across to the bedroom, Robert behind me. Once in the bedroom he quickly took off his clothes and went under the covers. I did the same. That night we spent loving each other until dawn. We slept for a while until I awoke and feeling hungry, got out of bed and put on my dressing gown. I pulled out of the linen closet Daddy's old silk dressing gown neatly folded and threw it at Robert for him to wear. I then stepped out of the bedroom to prepare some coffee and breakfast. I felt like a married woman already and knew that lovers like us could become married partners at the end.

Before switching on the kitchen lights, I went up to the window and saw a lot of snow on the ground and along the window sill. I also saw the face of a woman staring at me from the window pane. I withdrew in surprise . The face looked a lot like the face of Miss Stephanotis.

The image disappeared and I started to prepare coffee. I decided to make an American style breakfast with French toast and maple syrup. It had gone 7.30. am as I poured coffee into two mugs.

Then Robert showed up with wet hair. He had had

a shower.

He sat down at the table and I poured coffee for him and served out the French toast putting the bottle of maple syrup on the table. We both ate appreciating the sweetness of the French toast and the maple syrup.

"You may be able to get home today" I said.

"Well at least it's stopped snowing."said Robert. " I wonder if transportation will be available after the snowfall of yesterday" he said. Olivia put on the portable radio in the kitchen sitting on the side of the work surface. They listened to the news followed by the weather report on transport systems which were not yet up yet. There would be long delays. The temperature outside was -6degrees.

I told Robert about the face of the woman in the window pane. He told me to let him know if her face showed up again.

"I doubt I'll be able to get back home today" he said. "I hope it won't be too much for you to have me stay another day." he added.

After breakfast, they went to watch TV and tuned into the news program.

Chapter 5

Before switching on the kitchen lights, Olivia went up to the window and saw some snow flakes fall. But it wasn't snowing like yesterday. Shortly afterwards whilst she was preparing the coffee and the toast, it had stopped snowing.

"It's stopped snowing" said Robert.

"You may be able to get home today. The buses and trains are working." Said Olivia.

She put on her portable radio. They listened to the news followed by a travel report before the weather news came on

He got up from the table and withdrew in to the bedroom. He wanted to shave. He left the bedroom and went to Olivia who was washing up.

"Do you have a razor?" he asked her.

"Mmm. Yes, I have one in my sponge bag which is in the bathroom."

"Why do you need to use it? To shave?" she asked.

"That's it." He said

"Well, help yourself," she said to him.

While Robert was shaving, Olivia was finishing tidying up the kitchen and throwing the rubbish out. She then went to the dressing room to change in to clothes after a quick shower in the spare bathroom. As she was getting out of the shower, she heard the running feet again in the corridor. She quickly dried herself and left the bathroom to look around and see if she could see the running feet. There wasn't a soul in sight. She sighed with resignation as she went to her dressing room. She changed into a pair of black velvet trousers with a black jumper. She put on a pair of black slipper shoes. She sat at her dressing table and dabbed some make up on. As she left the bedroom, she peered out the window in the hall and saw to her surprise that it was raining. Robert was finishing off his shave.

"It's raining," she told him.

"Crazy weather," he explained.

Olivia went downstairs and opened the front door to test the weather. Yes it was raining. Then the snow was soon melting and the streets were clearing of snow. She knew it would be dirty and slushy to walk the streets now. By tomorrow, she would probably go back to work.

The alarm had been turned off at No.45. Olivia walked and passed it and checked to see if Reggie and Trevor had returned from the weekend. She would wait for Robert to come downstairs. She wondered once again about the face of the woman she saw in the window. She was inclined to think it was Miss Stephanotis, who she saw for the first time. She wondered if Miss Stephanotis had been in Reggie and Trevor's house over the weekend and set off the alarm. She wondered if something had been stolen. She would visit No.45 and see Reggie and ask her if everything was alright and ask if anything had gone missing. She would tell them about the face she saw in the window during the snowstorm of a few days ago. She was certain by now it was the face of Miss Stephanotis.

A quarter of an hour had passed and Robert came downstairs and joined Olivia in the sitting room.

"I'll be off today when it stops raining," he said.

"Let's see if the weather forecast is available and watch to see if public transport is working today."

They tuned into the news on TV. Yes, public transport was working. Some of the buses were slow and often delayed by the weather. His own train line was functioning as normal and he knew he'd get home without any particular problem. Within the half hour, the rain had stopped. It was now about 12 noon. They both got up and went to the front door, picking up their anoraks on the way. Robert opened the front door, letting Olivia out first. He slammed the door shut. After a brief explanation of the face in the window, the night of the snowstorm, Olivia told Robert that she wanted to stop at Reggie and Trevor's house at No.45 to check up on them and their house. Robert went with her. They rang the doorbell and soon after Trevor came to the door. When he saw them after opening the door, he said, "Oh, Hi. We've just come back from the weekend in Devon. We didn't know until we got home that the alarm had gone off."

"How is your house?" Olivia asked. "I was the one who notified the Police that the alarm had gone off. It was only yesterday that the alarm stopped ringing.

"Our safe was broken into and the money was

taken" said Trevor. "Some jewellery of Reggie was stolen but otherwise everything else is here, nothing else was stolen." He invited them both in. He called for his wife and when Reggie came downstairs she looked a bit hot and flustered. She had just been through her wardrobe and found a raincoat missing from her closet as well as two dresses and a pair of slacks and a top to go with it. She had phoned the Police who were on their way to take a Police report of the missing items.

Robert looked at his watch and thought how quickly time had passed. It was already 12.45pm. He told them he had not been home the whole weekend and excused himself, bidding bye for now as he got up to go. Olivia got up as well and they all made their way to the front door. Olivia waved goodbye as they left the house.

Robert carried on walking down the street to the Underground station while Olivia turned back to walk towards her house. Before they parted, they gave each other a warm embrace and kissed each other on the cheeks.

Chapter 6

As Olivia walked a short notice to her house, she developed a terrible backache. She had to stop walking momentarily until the pain was reduced. When she arrived home, her legs were so badly hurting that upon entering her home, she had to sit down on the hall settee. She took off her coat and placed it on the arm of the settee. She went upstairs to her bedroom and lay down on the bed covering herself with a light weight throw. She was soon asleep. She slept through for an hour. When she awakened her teeth felt dirty and she suddenly remembered hearing running feet again and someone quietly entering her bedroom. She lay on her bed for a while and eventually felt well enough to get up.

She went downstairs to the kitchen and made herself a cup of tea. While the kettle was boiling, she looked out the kitchen window and suddenly to her horror saw the face of Miss Stephanotis again.

She went to the garden door, unlocked it and stepped outside. She carefully looked everywhere for Miss Stephanotis and even called out her name, but it was to no avail. She couldn't find her anywhere. Having satisfied herself that she was not anywhere in the garden, she went indoors again, closing and locking the door behind her.

Just then the phone rang. She went to answer it. It was Robert who said he had arrived back in his flat and all was well. He told her he loved her and already missed her. She told him of the strange rest she had had and how her mouth felt dirty. She also told him about seeing Miss Stephanotis in her kitchen window.

"If it goes on like this, let me know," he told her. "I'll come back and stay with you until these ghosts go away" he said."When will you be going back to work?" he asked her. "Tomorrow she replied. "Well, I'll speak to you tomorrow to find out from you how the night went. Ring me anytime" he added. As they put their phones down,a cold strong wind blew the hedges in the garden. The wind subsided and relative peace fell on the garden.

In the evening when she had finished eating her dinner, Olivia cleared the plates and glasses. Afterward, she went to the sitting room and watched a movie on TV.

When it finished she got up switching of the lights and made her way upstairs to her bedroom. She changed into her nightie. She brushed her teeth, wiped her face with wam water and went to bed. It was about 10.30pm. She turned off the bedside light and curled up in bed and fell asleep.

In another part of town, Juanita had heard about the fabulous painting a certain Olivia Warren owned which hung in her living room. It was a Renoir painting.

It used to hang in the dining room of her parents house. They had passed it on to Olivia as she had no art on her wall in the sitting room. Juanita wanted this painting for her drugs.

Chapter 7

The following day, Olivia hurried herself to leave the house to go to work. She was an assistant to Thelma Goddard, Head of the editorial section of a famous fashion magazine, "Chic".

As she was leaving, she remembered to set the burglar alarm system. She then stepped outside, double locked the front door and turned and walked quickly down Sinclair Parade to take the Underground to Bond Street in the West End.

Her daily was due to come in today to clean the house. Her name was Nora. She had cleaned Olivia's house for five years and liked the job. She had to shop for Miss Olivia at the Grocery store and buy dinner for her, not to forget also a few things for breakfast. She had heard Miss Olivia talk about Robert a lot and knew they had a special relationship. She never probed into Olivia's life but knew instinctively that there relationship was one of love. They were very lucky to have found each other in this "wicked city" she thought. "God bless him" she prayed. Olivia kept her change and some pound notes inside a small tin box. Nora would take some money out of it as Olivia had asked her to do to pay for the groceries. It was a fine arrangement and worked well over these past five years. Nora stayed three to four hours a day laundering her clothes, sheets and towels. She prepared the chicken and left it on the side in the kitchen with cling film. She left the house at 1pm, closing the door behind her after turning on the alarm system.

It had stopped raining but the streets were very wet. There was flooding experienced by some people living by the Thames. Nora made her way to the bus stop and was soon off as her bus had arrived at the stop to whisk the passengers away.

At 3.30pm, Olivia's phone rang. It was Robert. "Are you busy tonight?" he asked. "I want a night alone." Olivia said.

"Must rush. Miss Goddard is ringing for me. See you tomorrow evening." She cried.

"She quickly put the phone down and with notebook and pen in her hand, she made her way to Room 17 to answer the boss's call. She spent the rest of the afternoon with Miss Goddard. When 5'oclock came, Miss Goddard told her she could leave. She got up from her chair and made her way to the door and left Room 17 to go back to her desk. She collected a few papers she had been working on and walked across to the lockers where she found her coat and handbag. She took the elevator to the ground floor and walked quickly out of the building.

In the Underground, on bard a train, she wondered what Nora had prepared for her for dinner that night.

Soon as she had arrived back at Sinclair Parade and opened the front door, she thought how clean and fresh the house smelt.

After dinner and a few glasses of wine, Olivia tuned in to the news programme and watched it for a time. She felt tired suddenly and knew it was time to get ready for bed.

She cleaned herself and changed into her bed clothes. She got in to bed, turned off the bedside lamp and crashed out.

At about 11.45pm, there were footsteps along the secret staircase. Someone was coming inside the house. Olivia was too tired to care about this. She wanted to sleep. Security told her that someone was in the house looking at her French painting in the sitting room. Drowsily, she got out of bed and quickly went downstairs and into the sitting room. She saw someone moving in the room but was so silent, she couldn't detect if it was a man or a woman. When she turned on the light, everything appeared good and normal. The Renoir was still hanging in the same place where she had originally put it. She checked the sitting room and everything was still there. She checked the dining room and nothing had been taken. Not worried anymore, she left switching off all the lights. She went upstairs and went up to bed. Soon, she was asleep. She heard nothing more and saw nothing. When she awoke at 6am the next morning, her mouth hurt her. She turned on the light, went to the bathroom, opened her mouth in front of the mirror and saw that some of the skin of her mouth was cut and bleeding. Her hands had become swollen and painful. There were marks on her arms and legs. Her eyes were red. In fact, she hardly recognised herself. She splashed some water on her face. She would wash her hair today.

Juanita had attacked her fiercely and before she left, she vowed she would have Olivia's Renoir.

Chapter 8

Two days had passed. Overnight, Olivia experienced being force fed with what tasted like gluten. She was awake enough to detect poison being administered to her to drink.

She felt dizzy and groggy the next morning but determined to keep her job..She showered, changed and put her make up on, leaving the house for the Underground station. By the time she got to the office of Chic magazine,she felt revived and better from the short walk and fresh air.

When she got to her desk, she saw Angie and said "goodmorning" to her. Angie helped Thelma Goddard with the clothes and models. Today, there was to be a fashion show headed by Chic magazine at Harrods starting at 3pm.The transporters were busy taking the racks of clothes downstairs to the waiting vans to drive them to Harrods store. Thelma Goddard was already there checking the lights with the electricians and looking over the range of make up for the models. The catwalk was being erected. The first floor was thriving and busy. It was now 12.30pm. Olivia had invited Robert to the fashion show. He said he would come and be there by 2.30pm. Until then, Olivia did many errands for Miss Goddard like buying a mixed salad for her for lunch from the canteen. At lunchtime many ate at the canteen including Olivia who ate a beetroot salad.

After a short lunch break everybody was back at

work. At 1.30 the models showed up. Their hair had already been done at Herberts the hairdresser in the West End. The makeup artists had just arrived putting their make up on racks with wheels. The models were busy trying on shoes to see if they fit them. One of the models was already having her face done by the make-up artist

A dozen bottles of champagne arrived and everyone on the set was given a glass.

The rest of the bottles were put into a portable fridge. Jean Francois the designer of the clothes arrived looking sleek and elegant in black. He greeted Thelma Goddard. She drank a toast to him for the marvellous collection, and both drank their champagne.

At 2.30 the models were putting on the clothes, their make- up touched up. They were nearly ready.

Robert arrived for Olivia and both were glad to see each other again. The guests were quickly arriving as they took and sat on their numbered seats facing the cat walk. One of the guests was Ivana Trump, first wife of Donald trump, former President of t he USA.

The fashion show went off successfully. Jean Francois was acclaimed a great designer. After the show, he thanked all who had made it possible for him to have the successful fashion show it had turned out to be.

"What did you think of the show? asked Olivia to Robert. "Fabulous" he said." A great success". He was watching the show amongst the audience. He had a good seat. He could see everything. Olivia had to stay behind the scenes in the background together with Jean Fencois's staff.

Everybody left the first floor of Harrods at 6pm either to go home or out to dinner.

Olivia and Robert went out to a French restaurant near Harrods. After dinner they stepped out into the chilly night air to flag down a black taxi. They found one eventually and drove back to Olivia's house. Before going upstairs to the bedroom, they both looked at the Renoir which had so far not been touched.With a sigh of relief, Olivia made her way upstairs followed by Robert. They had love and they both went to sleep after.

Nobody came in through the secret passage that night or bothered Olivia for her French painting. In the morning, Robert was the first to awaken. He left the bedroom to shower and shave. Olivia woke up about half an hour later, looked at her watch that said 7.30. She went in a hurry to the kitchen to put the kettle on. Through the kitchen window she could see out and knew that it was to be a beautiful morning.

Chapter 9

There was a sudden change in Olivia's life. Robert had become more distant with her and wasn't so loving to her anymore.

It was while Olivia was downstairs preparing breakfast one day, he awakened to see Juanita shooting something into his arm. She did this several times. He was asphyxiated and couldn't get out of bed. He heard Olivia call for him from the kitchen, and though he tried to answer, his voice was suddenly very weak and not audible.

Olivia came upstairs and when she entered the room, she immediately guessed that Juanita had been shooting their heroin into him. Olivia sat on the side of the bed and tried to comfort him. She gave him a sip of water, and he eventually recovered enough to sit up in bed. "I'd better tell the office I'm not coming in today or tomorrow due to illness" he said. After this, he wanted to go back to sleep. He was tired. Olivia helped him lie down comfortably and on her way out of he room said "I'll bring you up some breakfast." He lay back against the pillows. Soon Olivia arrived with a tray of hot coffee with milk and toast with butter on it and some jam in a small dish. There was a small glass of orange juice. She put the tray on his lap He took the cup of coffee and sipped it.It was the perfect breakfast for him' He began to feel better. Olivia was sitting by his bed on a bed-room chair.

She took her mobile out of her dressing gown

pocket and phoned her NHS surgery. She booked an appointment for 9.45 this morning. She would take Robert to see her own doctor and ask him for methedrine, explaining what had happened to her boyfriend. She herself would not be able to go to work that day.

She felt hatred for Juanita and prayed someone would avenge her the foul deed. Her doctor would have understood her feelings.

After Robert had eaten his breakfast, he told her that the shots on his arm had been going on for a few weeks, that Juanita wanted him to be her boyfriend. He had done all in his power to prevent this from happening. He confesed he had no love for this drug addicted woman and that he loved only Olivia.

They had plans to go away together, he and Olivia,and go to the South of France for the sun, the good food and good wines. They planned to go in a month's time. They had been looking forward to it . The only thing that could stop them would be Juanita and her interference in their lives.

Chapter 10

It cannot be disclosed what was said at the doctor's office except that Robert was given a renewable prescription for methedrine. After seeing the doctor, they took the prescription to the chemist who gave it to them together with disposable syringes. They took a taxi back home where Olivia helped administer the methedrine to him.

Miss Stephanotis who had been watching these proceedings decided to seek justice for both Robert and Olivia. That night, she had a lobotomy carried out on Juanita while she slept a few hours. It was not a complete operation, but enough to upset Juanita. There was no actual surgery done but it was technical and invisible and the operation was a success. Miss Stephanotis had been a doctor once, but nobody knew that she had lost her license to practise because of her terrorism.

That night all was quiet and peaceful and Robert slept well.Olivia next to him in bed also had a few hours of peaceful rest. Both woke up at 7 and feeling better.

Juanita had lost a lot of her memory and intelligence. Nobody would have guessed that she had been operated on.

This is how Robert and Olivia had been avenged. Miss Stephanotis was due a payment of money.

Olivia would take it up with her bank once Robert was over the worst.

The month passed quickly and soon it was time to take the flight to Nice.

When the morning came to depart for the airport, Robert came by taxi to collect Olivia at home. Olivia had a small case. She didn't bring much with her.

Juanita was nowhere to be seen. Robert guessed that she was a first class passenger. "I'll take care of this once we're back at the hotel." he said to himself

They were in their seats buckling up. A few minutes later, the airplane was moving. Soon after, they were ready for take off. The plane accelerated down the runway and lifted off. Soon they were in the sky.

Two hours later, they were flying above the Cote d'Azur. They would soon reach Nice airport in a matter of a few minutes.

Once on the ground, the plane stopped and the passengers were told to get ready to exit the aircraft. Once out of the plane, waiting buses took them to the terminal where they would all get out and assemble in front of passport control.

Olivia and Robert collected their luggage and made their way outside to wait for a free taxi. They asked the driver to take them to Holiday Inn Hotel in Nice. The taxi went off. So this was the Cote d'Azur thought Robert. "Oh, it's so exciting to be back here " said Olivia. It had gone 3pm.

At the hotel, they found their room which

overlooked the sea and garden. They unpacked and had a shower. Olivia with her bathrobe on, went to bed.After he had showered, Robert followed her to bed. They turned on the TV and watched a French movie in French. As neither of them spoke much of the language, they changed channels and watched an English speaking news program. After watching the news, they both fell asleep. When they awakened, it was past 6pm. They had been asleep , for three hours!

After dinner at a nearby seaside restaurant,a short walking distance away from the hotel, they went back to their hotel and to their room. Robert stayed dressed while he watched TV. When Olivia came out of the bathroom, Robert told her he had some business to attend to in town and would be back shortly. He secretly went to Juanita who was also staying at the same hotel. He arrived at the door of her room and knocked on it. She opened the door and let him in. She did not wish to return to London as Robert had asked her to do. She took him in her arms and tried to kiss him but he withdrew from her and said " I love Olivia, I don't love you." At this, Juanita grabbed a knife from the fruit bowl and lunged it into his shoulder. Stupified, Robert ran out of the room. Just then, someone from hotel management knocked at the door and stepped in the room. He had witnessed the attack. He asked Juanita if she was alright. She just nodded. He stayed in the room until the Police showed up. He told them what he had witnessed. They arrested Juanita and drove her to the station

In the morning she would know better if she was allowed to continue her stay in France.

At the Reception, Olivia got hold of a First Aid Kit to dress Robert's wound. The police passed by and saw Olivia dressing his wound. They soon left after a few questions had been answered. They found out that Juanita had followed them from London to the hotel and had booked herself in. No, she was not a relation and she wasn't a friend. A drug dealer and head of a South American drug cartel, she was extremely wealthy, able to have anything she wanted. She could pay for a war. The Police left after these preliminary questions.

Robert helped himself to some more beer from the mini bar. He lay on the bed trying to relax. Olivia was by his side. The nightmare was over. They kissed each other in spite of Robery's pain on his shoulder. They would spend a lovely holiday with each other and forget Juanita. The police may send her back to London on an extradition order.. She would have to face British Police there.

Olivia and Robert would never forget this holiday of a week, and yet one thing that worried them was Juanita's money. She was bribing everybody with it. Would Olivia and Robert ever get through the troubles Juanita gave them? Would she pay money out to be cleared of crime?

Robert and Olivia could love each again in spite of Robert's pain on his shoulder. When the morning came, they both awakened to a new day and being together was the best they felt they could have. Dressing his wound, Olivia told Robert that she loved him. Robert kissed Olivia and said 'I love you til the end of time.'

After getting up and changing, they both decided to spend the day in Monte Carlo, twenty minutes away by car. They noticed a lot of jewellery shops there and walked into one shop.They found a wonderful diamond ring which fit the finger of Olivia.

Being a good diamond it was expensive. Robert paid for it and Olivia kept the ring on. They walked out of the shop overjoyed by the purchase. They went to the main café of Monte Carlo and ordered a glass of champagne to celebrate.

Later on in the evening, Robert asked her to set a date for the wedding. After a good dinner at one of the restaurants in Monte Carlo, they got a taxi and went back to their hotel in Nice. The ring had changed everything and there was new meaning to their love for each other. Olivia started making plans and decided they would live together in Robert's flat. She decided to move out of her house and sell it. Many plans, many changes but their affection for each other never changed. Happily they went back to their hotel room. They laughed with happiness. It was to be the beginning of a new life and the end of their single lives.

HARBOUR ISLAND

Chapter 1

The Plane landed on the runway and cruised on the tarmac.

The loudspeaker on the plane said they had arrived at Nassau International Airport.

The passengers stood up and collected their belongings from the hold above their heads and proceeded to put on their jackets. Soon, they were all ready to leave the plane and stood in single file waiting.

It wasn't long before they had left the aircraft and were making their way to the terminal for passport control, immigration and then customs. Eventually, they collected their luggage and made their way out of the terminal. They went out of the building and stood for a while waiting for the taxi to be available to take them to their destination in Nassau.

Those who remained at the airport were making a connection to another island. They made their way to check in and walked to Gate 3 where they could sit and wait for the plane due to take them two hours away.

Two hours had passed and there was no sign of an airplane to take them to Harbour Island. Roger had asked at the desk how long the delay would be. "There's a lot of traffic on the runway at Eleuthera.

We can guess it will be another hour late," said the airline steward to Roger. We will keep a lookout for the radio contact and we will let you know further about your departure to Harbour Island." she said.

It had gone 5 o'clock and still there was no sign of the plane. Suddenly at 6pm the loudspeaker asked all the passengers on Bahamas Air flight 320 to get ready to embark. The tired passengers waited in a queue. Finally, they slowly made their way to airplane parked outside. The buses took them to their plane where the stairway was ready from them to ascend to the entrance of the plane. Once in, they found their way to their reserved seats on the plane.

All the passengers were now seated with their seatbelts on and their seatbelts on with their coats and luggage in the compartments above their heads. Soon the plane closed its' doors and eventually the airplane moved slowly to their take off. About twenty minutes later, a loudspeaker sounded and a member of the crew told the passengers to get ready to disembark as the plane approached Eleuthra Airport. Fifteen minutes later, they were flying in the sky to arrive at Harbour Island Airport. There were five passengers left on the airplane. Roger and his family were ready for disembarkation. The plane came to a halt and they went to queue to get off the flight. The last in the queue was travelling alone.

They were taken by small bus to the terminal. They got off and walked quickly to Passport Control and Customs. They were soon in the courtesy bus on the way to Harbour Island Hotels. They got off the bus when it reached the hotel.

Roger checked in and they were soon escorted to the rooms that had been reserved for them. Roger and Nancy shared a room in the suite and the children were put into the second room next to their parents. There was a spacious living room with a television. There wasn't much time for unpacking. They all obeyed their travel clothes and trainers and put on something for the evening. When they were ready, the four of them left the suite and walked across to the dining area which was outdoors. They were shown a table. Roger ordered a drink and Nancy to. They soon had their drinks in hand, reading the menu at the time. There was Caribbean music on whilst they dined. After dinner, a local singer came with his guitar. The music had been turned off as he prepared to perform his songs playing on his guitar. There was half a moon and the evening could not have been more agreeable. He sang "Yellow Bird" which was one of Nancy's favourite songs. He sat at their table for another fifteen minutes whilst Roger asked for the bill. He signed his name and wrote down the room number on the invoice. They got up from the table and said good night to the waiter. Roger tipped him, gladly accepted by the young man. They continued walking until they had reached their suite.

They said their goodnights and sleepily went in to their room. Roger stayed on in the living room and went to the mini bar when he helped himself to gin and tonic.

He then went across to the television and turned it on. He automatically switched in to CNN News which he kept on. He rang room service to ask for some ice. He than sat down on the armchair to watch the news. New England had a lot of snowfall and people living there could hardly leave their houses. Their cars were stuck at the snowdrift. It continued to snow. Suddenly, there was a knock on the door. Roger went to open the door for room service. The waiter came in and put the large bucket of ice on the shelf in the mini bar. When done, he retuned to leave, only to be stopped by Roger who gave him a tip. He said goodnight to the waiter and watched him leave the suite. He then took his glass of gin and tonic, crossed over to the bar and put three ice cubes into the glass. He returned to his chair and sat down, sipping his drink and continued watching the news. There was a sudden bulletin. A convict from Fulsom Prison had escaped. He was last seen in Miami. The Police believe he may be on the way to Cuba or make a hasty retreat to the Bahamas. The newsroom showed a photograph of Eric Thomas. Roger remembered the face in the photo. He was the fifth passenger on the plane that had brought them to Harbour Island.

Roger finished his drink and suddenly feeling very tired he decided to turn in. It was past midnight. He walked across the room of the front door and locked the door. He turned round and made his way to the bedroom. He opened the bedroom door. There was a blue night light on and he could see that his wife was asleep. It was a warm nigh with not a cloud in the sky as he closed the curtains. In a short while, he was ready for bed. He locked the bedroom door and lay his head on the comfortable pillows. It wasn't long before he was asleep. The night sky was lit by the half moon, passing its' rays on the dark night. All was quiet and at peace. Sleep overtaking the visitors of Harbour Island Hotel. The day would soon break. Another busy day would begin.

Chapter 2

Three days had passed without incident in spite of Eric Thomas' presence on the island. The children, Toby who was eleven years and Miranda, 9 years had discovered snorkelling and finding beds of coral in the sea. Their parents, Roger and Nancy sometimes went with them to view the corals under water and were as amazed as the children to see so many of them. After lunch, they went back to their places on the beach and excitedly dipped themselves in the salt water and walked along the shore. After an hour, they went swimming. Their faces and bodies were getting suntanned. They looked the picture of health. When they went snorkelling again in another area, they could see a lot of conk shells underneath the water. The large grey shells were often seen for sale in a few shops in town together with other shells. Roger encouraged his children to start collecting shells and keep them at home as decorations. They tried conk soup for lunch one day as they sat at a table at the side of the bar by the beach. "It's not bad" said Nancy. The children took to it and ended up eating it for lunch every day until they left to go back home.

When they left the beach, they usually went back to their cottage to prepare for the evening. Once they went to the small boutiques next to the hotel where jewellery, clothes and decorations for the home were sold.

Nancy found a nice bracelet made in France. Roger bought it for her. In another boutique where they sold mirrors surrounded by shells, Nancy chose a large mirror to go into their bathroom at home. She chose two other mirrors to go into their bedrooms and these were surrounded by shells. The total price came to $180 dollars. Having paid, the Family walked back to their cottage. Mirrors would be posted to their home in Long Island that February day. Rose, the Housekeeper would take them in.

A few evenings later, Roger walked his family to the local disco after dinner. There was loud disco music coming from the club. As they made their way to the entrance, they were stopped by a doorman who told Roger and Nancy that the children were not permitted in to the club. Disappointed, they were all forced to retreat and go back to their rooms in the hotel.

Once in their cottage, the children turned on the TV and after strolling through the lists of programmes opted for a comedy, "The Man in Mars".

At 11.30pm, the children went to bed. Nancy had returned to bed earlier and Roger knew she was soundly asleep. He then turned off all the lights in the living room except the small overhead light in the sitting room. He locked the door and made his way in to the bedroom. Soon, he was in bed.

The night passed by peacefully in Suite 598 when suddenly there was a noise that awakened both Nancy and Roger. Someone was trying to force the front door open. Roger quickly got up, picking up his dressing gown. He rushed out of the bedroom, switching on all the lights. By the time he opened the front door, there was nobody there. Turning on the outside light, he walked carefully around the cottage but saw nothing. When he got back to sitting room, his wife was in the kitchen preparing some coffee. He looked at his watch. It was now 4pm. The children sat on the sofa wondering what was going on. Roger told them that an intruder tried to open the front door that had been locked. They had run away. Roger never caught him. He persuaded Toby and Miranda to go back to bed.

After drinking Nancy's coffee, Roger got changed and walked outside. It was 5.15am and was getting brighter with the forecast of a sunny day. He walked towards the main part of the hotel. Everything was calm, not a sound could be heard.

As he walked, he suddenly saw something glittering on the ground where his feet were. He stopped and bent down to pick it up. When he got up with the glittering piece in his hand, he saw it was a broach. It looked real. Could it be a real diamond, pearl and ruby broach? He asked himself. He clutched the broach in his hand. The only person around at that hour of the morning was security.

He decided to find out if Eric Thomas was still living in the house next to the hotel. It was a short distance away. As he walked, he sensed that someone apart from Security at the hotel was watching him. He suddenly saw the house that was in front of him. There were no lights on. He only supposed that the occupants of the house were still asleep. As he stood there, hidden by bushes and trees, he heard the purring of an engine of a car. About one minute later, a car drove up. The driver got out of the car. It was Eric Thomas. The passenger was a man related to Eric, possibly his father. They both looked around. There was quiet. Nothing stirred. Satisfied, they both climbed up wooden stairs until they got to the porch and went inside the house. A few lights went on in the house. The upstairs lights were on and Roger could just make out the two men going to the bedroom. A few minutes later, one of the bedroom lights was turned off. Than the lights of the second bedroom was switched off. Suddenly, it started to shower. Roger thought he better move on and go back to the hotel, and to his room. As he turned to go, lightning struck then a few seconds later, torrential rain came down. He continued on his path quickly and about ten minutes later, he was in his Suite 987. Shivering, he went to his room to shave and change his clothes. Outside, the waves of the sea rolled back and forth. The waves were getting higher, crashing on the shore. Roger turned on the television and eventually the weather forecast came on. They expected rain in the early morning today but the sky would clear by the afternoon and it would be sunny and bright with a wind. His wife awakened the children at eight and as they got up they changed in to shorts, shirts and jersey jackets. They went into the sitting room where they greeted their father who was still watching television. In spite of the rain, all four ventured outdoors and made their way to the indoor dining room. Nancy was using one umbrella from the suite whilst the children ran towards the reception desk sheltered by a roof. After breakfast, they wondered what they could do to pass the time in the wet weather. They knew it would stop raining in the afternoon. Until then, they would enjoy a good breakfast.

Chapter 3

By 11.30am, the rain had gone and the sun was now shining. Roger Saunton was an Englishman who had come to the States twenty years ago. His wife Nancy was from New York City.

Although he was happy enough to live in the city, he appreciated their house in the Hamptons more, where they went each weekend on National holidays.

He and his family usually went to England for ten days in the summertime to visit his mother who lived in the small house outside of London.

He worked in the fashion industry and supplied the store Bloomingdales with French perfumes.

That evening in the news there appeared a photograph of Eric Thomas from twenty years ago. The News report continued to explain how he had committed robbery and the murder of a woman in a Manhattan town house. He had murdered her for her jewels that she kept in a hidden safe and she and her son were the only ones in the house. The son had managed to set the alarm. The Police came quickly. In the meanwhile, Eric Thomas and his collaborator put the jewels and stashed them in a grey bag and made a hasty retreat through the door at the back of the house. When they opened the door and stepped out, they were met by Policemen. They were immediately arrested and put in a Police car to be driven to the station. An Ambulance had been called. It soon arrived and the body of the lady taken to the local hospital. The son went with them. Later on that morning, it was all over for Eric Thomas. The hospital notified the Police that Mrs Walton had died. This was relayed in the early evening news. Eric Thomas was charged with first degree murder caused by gunfire. He will go to a Prison for this and stay there for a certain amount of time. The relatives of the deceased were notified. Mrs Walton's son phoned many of them or sent emails to let them know what had happened.

Roger wondered how safe the hotel was, thinking that Eric Thomas may repeat the same offence here on the island.

Chapter 4

Roger had forgotten about the broach he lad picked up from the ground that morning he saw Eric Thomas in the villa next to the hotel. He took it out of his coat pocket and went across to his wife and showed it to her. "Where did you find this?" she asked surprised by the jewel. "It's mine" She said to him. I lost it years ago from a bank vault where I kept all my jewels. "It was a present from Daddy to Mummy and passed on to me shortly before our wedding. I never wore it."

"Let us put it in the safe where it will be perfectly safe" said Roger to Nancy. "Well, I am glad to have seen the broach again and look forward to wearing it New York once we are back."

Calling the children, the family left the suite and locked the door leaving the outside light on. The couple enjoyed drinking one of the bohemian cocktails served in the shells of coconuts and the children had Coca –Cola or orange juice. Eventually, after finishing their drinks they got up to dine in the outdoor area. After being seated, they were handed large size menus. After looking over the menu, Roger opted to eat a fish that was a favourite of the hotel and Nancy chose a fish that had been caught that day locally. The children chose to eat hamburgers. Roger and Nancy chose some vintage

Californian white wine to drink with their meal. The children had water. After dinner had been eaten, they got up from the table and made their way to their suite. When they arrived in front of the door, they noticed the front door was open and not locked. As they entered, everything was in place. Roger looked at the safe and noticed the outside door was open. He and Nancy quickly went over to the safe and unlocked it. To their amazement, the broach had not been touched. One of the pouches where the rings were kept had been handled. Nancy went through the rings and discovered her Hong Kong Jade ring was missing. She went through her other two pouches of jewellery to conclude that only the jade ring was missing. It was an emerald jade and held special memories for her, her mother and father. The burglary could have been worse. Nancy was grateful but nothing else had been stolen. They would report the burglary to the manager in the morning. The manager and his wife would have already gone home. It was too late to speak to them. After the shock of the burglary, they all sat down around the television and watched the tail end of the News.

After this, they watched Starsky & Hutch which finished at a quarter to midnight. They all went to bed afterwards. Roger double locked the door, keeping the outside porch light on, he then returned to his bedroom and got ready for bed. The sky was clear that night. They had not trouble falling asleep and slept soundly to seven. Nancy slept on and Roger knew his children would sleep on this morning.

As usual, Roger got dressed in old clothes and went out for his usual walk around the grounds of the hotel. He walked directly this time to the house next door which housed Eric Thomas and one other. He stopped short his walk and hid himself in the undergrowth watching the movements of the occupants of the rented villa. Another car was parked by the house and two men were emptying out their van carrying sack of something, "probably drugs" he thought to himself.

He watched the two men when suddenly Eric Thomas came out of the house to tell the men he did not want anymore bags. He gave them money in envelopes and they thanked him and moved on their van. They drove out of the driveway of the villa. It was now a little after eight.

No sooner had the van left then a car pulled up. A woman got out of the car. She was of medium height and medium build with light hair. She was good looking. When Eric Thomas saw her, he greeted her saying "Sally, how have you been? I'm up here on the porch." Looking up, she saw him and smiled. She climbed up the stairs to join him on the porch. Bob, the man who brought her to Harbour Island joined them. "How was the flight?" asked Eric to Bob. "Okay, I guess" replied Bob. "Good" said Eric. "Come in and have coffee with me" said Eric to Sally and Bob. The three of them went indoors, slamming the door behind them. At 11.30am that morning, two black youths arrived at the door. Sally opened the door. They asked for Eric Thomas. They had been sent by Lucien Sliver who was a drug dealer. They waited by the door whilst Sally went to speak to Eric. She returned and took them to Eric who was standing by the drinks bar. After introducing themselves as Show Boy and Pete, they said

"You wanted to deliver some goods to the main island. We've come to pick them up for delivery in Nassau."

Eric said "Yes, that's right." He walked a short distance to a door on the ground floor and opened the door with keys. He beckoned the two youth to follow him to the room where the plastic bags were located. They began taking the bags to the shoreline where ski jets were located. They stuffed the bags into compartments on the ski jets. They were limited in how many they could take. Afterwards, they were given money by Eric who told them to return to him tomorrow at the same time. They jumped on their speed jets and sped off.

Pleased with themselves, Eric Thomas knew he had made a great deal of money that day. It would be at the break of the new dawn the two courier boys would be back to collect some more of the contents in the plastic bags. Until then, Eric Thomas felt assured that the Bahamas could bring him the fortunes of a drug baron and he could settle down in the expensive house he always dreamed of.

Chapter 5

Early next day, Toby and Miranda awakened to what would be a beautiful day. They decided to go the beach for an early morning swim. After changing in their swimsuits, they quietly left the cottage and went towards the beach.

When they arrived there, they noticed two coloured youths scurrying "to and fro" on the beach, and then back to the villa rented by Eric Thomas. They walked to the shrubs where they could see better what the commotion was about.

Eric Thomas was in his dressing gown standing on the porch holding the front door open and the youths able to get to their ski jets faster to reload their cargo into the compartment of their ski jets. Suddenly, a shadow came over the children and a tall big man with big hands grabbed the children by their necks and forced them towards the house.

"Let go of me" cried Toby.

"You're hurting me as well" cried Miranda.

The big man dragged them to the house and up the stairs to a room. Toby was kicking the man and Miranda said, "You're hurting my neck. Stop it!"

When Eric Thomas saw them he told Gervaise to tie them up and put them in the spare room upstairs.

Gervaise gagged them with the spare her chief and bound their feet and hands with rope. Gervaise left them there without a word.

In the late afternoon, he returned with a bottle of mineral water and two glasses. He filled the glasses up with mineral water, taking off the gags on the thirsty children and let them drink. They finished the bottle. Miranda asked to be excused. When she returned, Toby went to relieve himself. Gervaise had released both their hands and feet. Gerviase tied them up again and put a her chief around their mouths. He then left, taking the empty bottle of mineral water with him. It was 6pm. Toby and Miranda thought they had heard a commotion by the front door. Toby could hear his father's voice and the voice of another man. Suddenly, Eric Thomas started screaming.

Voices were raised and a gun was fired. Silence fell. Julie had caught the stray bullet on her shoulder. They all heard a rumpus from upstairs and the door to the bedroom being attacked. Roger went upstairs and quietly located the room which was under lock and key. When he turned to go down again, Gervaise was behind him. He escorted the Policeman, a Sergeant Calloghan. He said, "The kids are here". He said no more. Eric Thomas told Gervaise to get the car, that they were leaving for the mainland. While Gervaise went out, Eric Thomas bound Roger and Calloghan to two chairs and gagged them both. They helped Julie up from the floor and together they left the house. Julie's would be not so serious; it was a scratch. She covered her shoulder with a shawl. Once in the car, they sped off to the airport. They would soon be on their way back to Nassau and then to freedom in the States.

Chapter 6

Nancy got up at the usual hour of 8am. After breakfast, she changed in to her swim suit and got ready to go out. This morning was an unusual morning. When she got up, there was nobody in the suite. She thought they had all gone down to the beach for an early morning swim. When she was ready to leave for the beach with its' pink sand, she was amazed that they were not there. There was no longer Toby, Miranda or Roger. May be they were snorkelling by the coral reef she thought. She knew she would find them. She put on her cap and walked into the water. There were a few people on the beach that morning. She swam a distance to where the corals lay hidden in the water. She could make out two figures looking at the corals underneath the water and made out that they were two young adult women. When she resurfaced, they also came up with their snorkels on.

"Hello" she said to them. "Do you come here often?"

"Oh yes" they replied, "We come here everyday."

Relieved by this news, Nancy asked "Did you see two children here by the corals this morning?"

"No, we did not see anyone here this morning" one of the girls replied.

"Usually there's a young boy and his sister that

come to look at the corals every morning

"But they never showed up today" the other girl explained.

"Well, if you see them, please tell them that their mother is looking for them and ask them to come back to the beach. I will be there." Then waving her hand at them, Nancy swam towards the beach.

Two hours later, Nancy decided to change her swimming costume and top. She went to the changing room and when she came out she had brushed her hair and changed into a black swimsuit and matching black and white wrap. She walked briskly towards the reception desk. She would tell the hotel receptionist that Roger, Toby and Miranda had not returned to the suite last night and was nowhere to be seen in the hotel or on the beach. She had checked the coral reef but the children were not there. She declared them missing.

"Can you phone the Police?" she asked Dina, the receptionist.

"When was the last time you saw them?" asked Dina.

"They were there last night and so was my husband" she answered. A telephone call went through to the Police. They would soon be at the Hotel.

Dina told Nancy to go back to her room and wait for them there. Half an hour later, there was a knock on her door. When she opened the door, Dina stood there with two Policemen. Nancy invited them in. She told them to sit on the sofa in front of the television. The Police asked a few question as to the time she last saw her family. After Nancy had answered all the questions, she said that her husband had mentioned that he saw Eric Thomas in the house next to the hotel. Eric Thomas was a well known criminal in the States. He had murdered a woman in her house in up town Manhattan. He did it for her money and her jewels. She had no idea why he came to Harbour Island. Her husband had mentioned two coloured youths on ski jets visiting the property. When the interview had ended, the two policemen thanked Nancy for her cooperation and told her they would be back that evening to give her that report. They then left with Dina on their way out. The Police told her not to worry and try to enjoy her day.

At 7pm, Nancy was about to leave her suite to dine at the outdoor restaurant, when there was a knock on the door. Police showed up with Roger, Toby and Miranda. "They were tied up in the house next to the hotel and gagged as well," said one of the Policemen.

"Oh, what a relief it's over" said Nancy.

"We're glad to be back," said Roger. "If it hadn't been the telephone call to the Police this morning, we would have been done for," said Toby.

"Eric Thomas was planning to return in a few more days and we wouldn't have had a chance to survive," said Roger. "Anyway, it's over now. I would like to have a shower and I expect the children would also like to shower and change."

"We'll meet you at the restaurant, unless you would prefer to wait for us here."

"I would rather wait for you here," she said. The Police told her that her information about Eric Thomas and what her husband told her about him gave it all away. It wasn't long before the Police found her family, bound and gagged in the house. They took their leave and went back to the station in their car.

Epilogue

Roger and the children were very glad to back in their hotel room. It wouldn't be long now before they would depart for NYC and the Hamptons. They had two day left of the holiday before they would fly back to the States. Roger told them that the weather was cold and snowy. Their holiday on the island with the shore of pink sand would remain in their memories for a long time to come. As Roger & Nancy walked along the shore, they remembered Eric Thomas momentarily and knew that his drug trafficking would never reach them in the Hamptons. They would start packing their bags, getting ready to leave the day after tomorrow. They had the mirrors surrounded by seashells as souvenirs of their stay there. Toby and Miranda wanted to come back to Harbour Island. Roger might consider it. In the meanwhile, the world seemed to be a wonderful place.

DOES CRIME PAY?

Chapter One

I departed by air to Nice on the Cote D'Azur, France for a four day break to get some sunshine, French food and wine. I also had a little shopping to do. I was with a male travelling companion who got us on to the flight because he is good with computers and filling in forms to enable us to travel.

We successfully left the country and flew to Nice. I was followed by Helen Aine of the IRA. She is an heir and I ften wonbdered why she followed me. I don't like her. She was not alone in flowing me. Amina also came and stayed in the same hote,l as us.. She stole one of my notebooks and set about writinga blook about Anwa (a Police marksman) who was also my security in my house. She grabberd this idea for herself. She is not a writer or authpr.

Amina stopped going to school aged 10. She later became a CIA agent and then got married to Afonso Nugent of the Colubian Fack leader who ran a drug cartel. Although they married, the marriage did not last long and she had hired a kiuller to assassinate him and took of her millions with her. She is very wealthy with drug money. She stole Anwa's attention from me fopr drugging him with heroin. She forced him to have a sexual relationship with her and forced him to accompany her to the first viewing of the last James Boond film, Not |Time To Die with Dainel C|raig.

Amina has taken over the security of this house

without being asked to. She attacks me every night. Recently she smashed my house with a mallet and ,medicated with a psychriatic medicine that she was meant to be taking. She is a cruel tormentor with no scruples for her activity. She is a bad person who can never be good to ,me, She drugs with heroin.

The Labour Leader, Sir Keir Starmer had hped that the money, the clothes would all go to Yuskiko who carries my passport which she stole from me last year. At this point in time, the various claimants of this money, I should have received fgrom these books. Everyone is fgighting hard to get hold of this money.

Julia is the U who married an American FBI man and she told him she wanted all the money and my books I had written. President Biden has become involved in this scandal and stole my notebooks and computer for her. This happended whilst I was having a shirt break in the South of Frnace. Julia' father was a diplomat working for the UK government. He was ambassafdor to Spain and after became British ambassador to Japan. He spoke fluent Jpanses. I met them at the embassdy in T|okyo They were very good people. I met their only daughter , Juia married to Seymour in London. They lived off th Fulhma Road at the time but later moved to Barnes.I believe Julia still lives there despite of the divorce between her and Seymour in the 90s.

Ucitation . He wa succful when I came through; I was having probles at the time with me

Seymour was banker who always wanted to have all the money in the world. She was the original thief who wore all my clothes and stole them. She is known to be a whore and works for the sex and the money. She is the Jew and the U.

Gunran Agnew, a Korean woam always wants my writing.She accesses my house via the Secret Passage and locates my compter case and steeals my computer. She is now trying to claim that she wtote this book. The government agent picked her up from a Seoul brothel and brought her across to England. She took over the Secuirty of the video whiuch show what is going on in London. She gets paid fo it. She publuished my book several years ago, a case of civil dispoendiance that a literary aagent had mistaken her for me and paid her for the book. She was paid very generously. Otherwise she is a whore and a prostitie,. Rhey paid the wrong person and didn't realise this whrn tey had returned to London with the money.

Due to the Secret pAssage my life was saved by Amwa. He was my ecurity in my house. Whilst I stopped breathing whilst I was asleep in my bed. I was dead. He was so upset he tried to shake me to wake me up and gave me resuscaitain and gave me financial reasons. I believe he may have tried to kill me that night. When I went for my summer holiday in 2020 to Sarinia I was follwed there by drug dealers who tried to tek over the Airport.

Anwa spent a week safe guarding th Airport and supporint the hosilt Briths dealers from taking over the airport. Thos 2 incidents I owed Anwa several million poiunds. He never got apid that was a tragedy. After this, Anwa fell in to Amina's hands and was drugged for days on end. She gave him her dirty money and forced him in to bed with her. Eventually, he recovered himself. My good Doctors saw that he recovered.